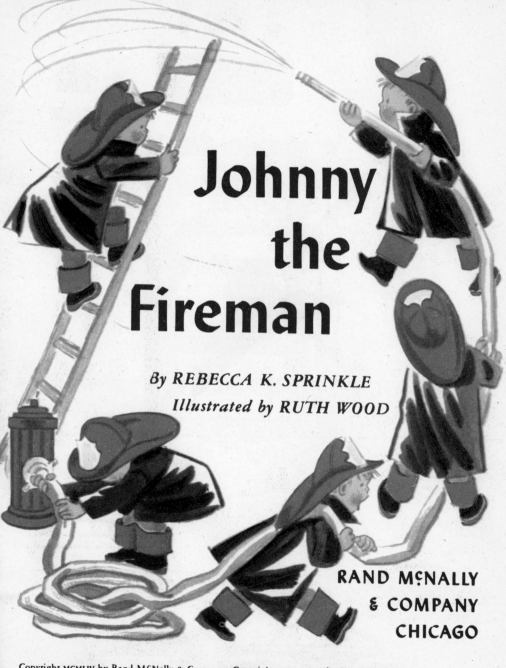

Johnny the Fireman

By REBECCA K. SPRINKLE

Illustrated by RUTH WOOD

RAND McNALLY
& COMPANY
CHICAGO

JOHNNY lived in a big apartment house in a big city. Around the corner there was a large fire station. When Johnny and his mother passed the fire station on their way to the grocery store, Johnny always looked in. He saw many fire engines, bright and shiny red. He saw many firemen, spick-and-span in their blue uniforms. Everything and everybody was ready to put out a fire when one started.

As he skipped down the street toward the grocery store, Johnny always said to his mother, "When I'm big, I want to be a hardware-store man like Daddy. But I want to be a fireman, too!"

"I suppose you'll just have to decide," his mother
told him. "You'll have to decide which you want
to be most — a hardware-store man like Daddy,
or a fireman."

But Johnny couldn't decide.

The next summer Aunt Jane invited Johnny to
come for a visit. His mother and daddy took him
in the car and left him for two whole weeks.

Aunt Jane lived in a tiny little town in a tiny little cottage. Around the corner there was a fire station — a very small fire station. The first morning Johnny was there, he walked down to the station and looked in. There was one shiny, red truck. There was one fireman in a blue uniform.

"But where are the other firemen?" Johnny asked. "One fireman can't drive the truck and hook up the hose and turn on the water and get out the ladder and put out the fire!"

The fire chief smiled and said, "You just wait and see. Wait till there's a fire, and you'll find out!"

Johnny waited and waited. It seemed that there would never be a fire. Finally, the day before he was to go home, the fire whistle on top of the

firehouse hooted and tooted to warn everyone of
a fire. Johnny hurried out of Aunt Jane's tiny little
cottage and stood where he could watch. Now he
would see how one fireman could put out a fire!

But, as he watched, he saw several men suddenly running fast toward the firehouse. For when the fire whistle had started to blow, the butcher had dropped the pork chop he was cutting and dashed out of his store with his white apron flying in the breeze. He raced to the fire station.

The filling-station man rolled out from under the car he was greasing and went running toward the fire station without even wiping his hands.

The baker in the bakery pulled a pan of cinnamon buns out of the oven so that they would not burn. Then he dashed off to the fire station without taking off his tall white hat.

The cobbler left the shoe he was half-soling and raced out in his apron.

And the hardware-store man dropped the box of hammers he was unpacking and ran around the corner as fast as he could go.

All the men who had raced to the fire station now jumped onto the one bright, shiny, red fire truck. The fire chief in his blue uniform jumped into the driver's seat. He roared the motor and shifted the gears, and away the fire truck streaked up the street with the siren sounding.

Johnny raced along the sidewalk behind the fire
truck. He saw it pull up two blocks away where a
little store was sending out big puffs of gray smoke.

The fire chief pulled to a stop. The butcher
jumped out and began to unfasten the hose. The
baker attached the hose to the water hydrant. The

cobbler carried the hose inside and sprayed water on
the flames. The filling-station man got the ladder
off the truck and put it against the building. The

hardware-store man climbed the ladder and crawled in through the window. The fire chief was in charge and told each person what to do.

Suddenly the clouds of smoke disappeared. The hardware-store man stuck his head out the window and called, "All clear up here!"

The cobbler ran out the front door and called,
"All clear down here!"

Then they rolled up the hose and hooked up
the ladder and everybody climbed back on the
truck, for the fire had been put out.

Just then the fire chief saw Johnny standing and watching. "Hop up, Johnny," he called. "We'll give you a ride home."

The filling-station man swung Johnny up to the seat by the fire chief. The other men stood on the

sides and back of the truck. The chief roared the motor and shifted the gears. He turned on the siren so that Johnny could hear the nice, loud noise. And they streaked up the street and into the fire station.

Then all the men — the cobbler, the baker, the butcher, the filling-station man, and the hardware-store man — hopped off the truck and went running back to their regular jobs.

"Now you see what happens," the fire chief told Johnny. "In this little town we do not have enough money to pay several firemen to spend all their time waiting to put out fires. So we have *volunteer* firemen. They are men who offer to be helpers when

there is a fire. Most of the time they are the butcher, the baker, the cobbler, the filling-station man, or the hardware-store man. But when there is a fire, they are firemen!"

Next day Johnny's mother and daddy came to get him and take him home with them. After he had given them each a big hug, he told them about the volunteer firemen who help when there is a fire. He smiled at his mother.

"Now," Johnny declared, "I don't have to decide whether I'll be a hardware-store man or a fireman when I get big. For I'm going to live in a tiny little town like Aunt Jane's. Most of the time I'll be a

hardware-store man like Daddy. But I'll be a volunteer fireman besides so that, when there is a fire,
I can be a fireman, too!"